Copy #1 of 10.

The Hypocrite

Antony Szmierek

Copyright © 2018 Antony Szmierek

All rights reserved.

ISBN:
ISBN-13: 9781728789811

JUKEBOX AT THE AMSTERDAM

Young Turks - **Rod Stewart**

Invisible City - **Primal Scream**

Criticize - **Alexander O'Neal**

Rocket Man - **Elton John**

A Letter To Elise - **The Cure**

The Escapist - **The Streets**

Only You Know - **Dion**

Sunny Afternoon - **The Kinks**

Trash - **Suede**

Into The Hollow - **Queens of the Stone Age**

Standing At the Sky's Edge - **Richard Hawley**

How Soon Is Now? - **The Smiths**

In Your Eyes - **BadBadNotGood**

Space Song - **Beach House**

Clean Living - **The War On Drugs**

Hangout at the Gallows - **Father John Misty**

Four Out Of Five - **Arctic Monkeys**

Apocalypse Dreams - **Tame Impala**

Something To Remember Me By - **The Horrors**

Subhuman 2.0 - **Cabbage**

ANTONY SZMIEREK

THE AMSTERDAM

What brings you to The Amsterdam? I wasn't lucky enough to find a place like this on my first night in the city. No, I spent my first night in some horrible franchise pub watching football highlights on mute and pretending to read a book. And yes, it really was as sad as it sounds. You get brainwashed into thinking that pubs are these hotbeds of social activity but nobody really strays outside the group they came with or the conversations they're used to having. It makes everyone feel comfortable.

Let me go some way to giving you a better welcome than I had. Eddie, I'll have a pint of the usual and our friend here will have… will have the same! No, your money is no good for now. Welcome to Edinburgh.

Cheers.

I pay in cash because I'm so bad at saving money. I need a visual aid, you know? Quite tragic that I still haven't figured that out. Oh, there's a list. I haven't been to the dentist in four years. Most of the time if people send me a message I'll read it and never reply. I've ran away on multiple occasions because that's much easier than staying put and sorting things out. I keep secrets from myself - tell myself one thing and secretly desire another. I don't read any of the post that gets sent to me because it's always bad news. I get jealous and I have a superiority complex. There's a three to one ratio of the death of houseplants in my flat and the death of relationships I've tried to keep alive. Perhaps worst of all, and I'm only putting this on the table because I believe honesty is the best policy, but I make absolutely terrible decisions when drunk. I am, I guess, a hypocrite in every sense of the word.

Oh, and I have a tendency to overshare. But why talk about the weather or tourist attractions? We're not here long, we might as well talk about the things we really want to talk about. There's a table over there by the fire, actually. Now, I wouldn't want you to feel any undue pressure here but... shall we? So you noticed him too? Not the usual type we get in here, especially not at this time. I don't think I heard him say a word, did you? But yes I agree, there was something purposeful about the way he leaned on the bar. Would you say that pinstripe suit was expensive? I can never tell. Something about pinstripe reminds me of the rich in the eighties, but it's probably just unfashionable now. Maybe we'll pluck up the courage to ask where he's from after a few drinks. I think I hit my sweet spot at about three if I've eaten a good meal beforehand, probably at part way through the second if I've only managed a bowl of cornflakes. That happens sometimes with living above a pub. It's easier to sit down here and drink in the echoes of stranger's conversations than it is to be upstairs. The ghost voices that come through the floor make it feel like you've slipped into a parallel dimension.

What do you think of the place, anyway? A pub called The Amsterdam, pretending to be a Hungarian ruin bar, sitting quietly at the arse-end of Edinburgh's Royal Mile?

It does, doesn't it? It all just kind of makes sense. Minus four outside tonight if you believe the TV. No place I'd rather be.

You see Eddie, behind the bar? The big guy who's gut looks like he might sweep the pint pots off the bar if he turns around too quickly. Yeah that's him, in the Celtic shirt. Sort of bloke that you'd expect to work in a place like this if they weren't already a barber or a cabbie. He's done me a solid on the rent upstairs, and let's me get away with a bar tab he knows it's impossible for me to pay off. Great bloke. Well, this place has been in his family for generations. That's his old man on the wall over there with the pipe and the audacious grin. Just there, beside the 'No photos' sign.

Oh yeah, he enforces it.

It was his Dad's idea to make The Amsterdam a maze of trinkets and incongruities and Eddie just took the idea and ran with it. How it stays warm I'll never know. If you squint and know the right angle you can see the street outside through some of the cracks in the walls, and in a strong wind the whole place leans to the left, I swear. But maybe that's just a trick played on me by the alcohol. Besides, this is the real Edinburgh and I wouldn't have it any other way. Memories. Regrets. Souvenirs. A fucking bookshelf, for some reason. Who reads in a bar, anyway?

But this right here is the best spot in the house - a safe distance from the fire but close enough to still feel it's warmth, a short walk from the bar, and quite a good vantage point of The Man in the Pinstripe Suit. He doesn't seem to have a bag with him, does he? Can't have come straight from work. Maybe he just has a wardrobe full of that same suit over and over, like a villain in a cartoon.

You're right! Maybe he's waiting for someone. Anyway, it really is great to meet you. You're not here long, you say? I can give you some recommendations on places to eat and drink, sure… but for now good conversation is something I think will do us both good. I don't mean to be presumptuous, it's just you can only enjoy a place so much on your own.

I've been a few things but I guess most consistently I've been a teacher. English, mostly. Language, Literature, and then recently Philosophy, but only at a rudimentary level and mostly for my own interest. It's difficult to teach if you feel like you're still learning, you know? So I'm not a teacher anymore, or at least not a professional one. It's difficult to explain, but I reached this point in my life where everything just seemed to lose its shape. Every time I had an idea, every time I set myself a goal, every time I thought I had this whole thing figured out, there'd be some crushing antithesis that'd chip away at me until the idea didn't exist anymore. Now, of course I don't want you to ring The Samaritans on my behalf, you needn't look so concerned. This isn't a cry for help. I'm bringing this up is because I'm confident that you will have experienced some of the same feelings.

Why else would you be here?

I should explain. I'm a sociable person and yet I'm aware of how deeply I value being alone. I cherish the memory of being in love - as

I believe I once was - and yet I know I'll still be unhappy when I eventually find somebody to share that feeling with again. Above all, I carry an overwhelming urge to make my mark on a universe that apathetically shrugs at the very notion of my existence. Life can be a cruel joke sometimes, you and I know that. It's a game that's impossible to win because it's rigged against the player. And yet here we are, searching for purpose and meaning just like everybody else.

There was a time that I could rationalise all this to myself because I knew I was a good person. I knew that deep down, no matter how bad things became, I deserved to be happy and would be happy eventually because the universe, somehow, would reward me for being fundamentally good.

I helped elderly people carry their shopping. I used my manners. As a teacher I would console my students if they were in pain and strive to make the world better for them. I lent people money. Offered chewing gum to strangers on the tram. Smiled at people I didn't know on the street and offered small talk and humour just in case they were lonely. If I passed the homeless I would give them my change. You get the idea, anyway. I'm not bragging, it's just that's how I lived my life. The problem with karma as a concept is that it's impossible to prove and yet it's taught and reinforced by almost everything and everyone. Religion is it's source, of course. It doesn't matter if you call it karma, the Commandments or Islamic Law. We know from being a child that if we do good things we will receive good things in return. Maybe we'll get an invitation to an afterlife. Maybe we'll be reincarnated as a king or a God. Maybe if we're polite to our Maths teacher we'll receive a higher grade in our end of term exam. Who knows?

And of course, our parents or guardians reinforce these ideas too. You begin life as the most special little human being that has ever lived. You are lavished with attention. You are told that no matter what, you are loved unconditionally. You are special. You matter. Whatever life is, congratulations! Against all odds, you are the protagonist. You are the goodie and other people are the baddies. When you are eventually old enough to be able to read or take in the plot of a movie, you see that the good guys always win, and naturally you put yourself in the hero's shoes, don't you? Because that's life, right there on the screen, and everybody wants you to win.

The problem with all of this, of course, is when you realise that you're probably not a good person. Nobody is, really. That girl you've always liked who is madly in love with someone else? He probably isn't cheating on her. He isn't manipulating her to get at the family fortune, either. He loves her too, but that isn't going to stop you trying to prise her away from him, is it? And that guy at work you've always been jealous of? His Dad isn't a major shareholder in the company, he just caught a few lucky breaks or, God forbid, worked hard. I must apologise if I've come off a little overfamiliar. I suppose you would have left after my whole opening gambit though if you were easily spooked. The last thing I'd want to do is make you feel uneasy, it's just that I can tell you see a little of yourself in me. You can, can't you? Your lack of interruption goes a little further than wanting to be polite or just being thankful for a cold beer and a warm fire. And listen, I'm young. This isn't a lecture. I'm not trying to make you see the error of your ways - there's a shelf full of Dickens over there for that kind of thing. It's just that you seem like a good listener and I like to talk. I guess that's the teacher in me. Sharing a drink with a stranger is a criminally underrated form of therapy, you know. There's very little at stake, there's no exchange of currency, and there's no need for either party to share or listen other than because they actually want to.

Do I have time for another?

Always.

Just be sure to put it on my tab. If Eddie doesn't understand what you're getting at just say my name and point over here. Mine's a pint for now, cheers. And when you return, now that we've got to know each other a little, I'd like to tell you about the worst thing I ever did. That's how I got here, after all.

We're all running away from something, right?

ANTONY SZMIEREK

UPHEAVAL

That was quick! Maybe Eddie's taking a liking to you? No, you're probably right. It tends to be quiet this side of town on a week night anyway and it seems tonight is no different. You don't seem the kind of person to be easily spooked, and so I'll let you into a little of the history of this place. It's twenty quid for a guided tour out there so count yourself lucky.

Eddie took this place over from his Dad you see, the chap on the wall, but what I didn't tell you earlier is that he was heavily involved in all kinds of organised crime. You'd do well to keep this to yourself by the way, our Eddie isn't particularly keen on this being public knowledge. All kinds of wares would go in and out of that door you came through, and the more…questionable stuff would go out the back. It was a meeting point, if you will. I'm talking, well - I'll lower my voice a little, if you'd care lean in - prostitution, drugs, arms. All sorts of black market shit. Thing is, those kinds of misdemeanours aren't easily forgotten round these parts. Sure, years have passed and sadly Eddie's Dad has passed too. But still, reputation is heavier than air and it hangs over this place like a thunderhead. That 'no photos' policy doesn't seem quite so outdated anymore, does it? How do you think I got the flat upstairs so cheap?

You see that painting over there? Just there, beside the jukebox. Recognise it at all? That's a good guess, I knew not to underestimate you! It's Roman, yes, but it's not the God you're thinking of. It's a painting of Janus, the two-faced God of all sorts of things.

Beginnings, endings, transitions, even doors for goodness sake. It catches the eye, that's for sure. I've always liked the colours in it, kind of like an angry autumn. The way the faces, both of them, are drawn in this reddy-brown, and then the background seems to be just beyond your perception. You look hard at it, past the faces and into the distance, and that mash of orange and yellow and brown becomes whatever you want it to be. Sometimes when I've been drinking spirits I'll confess I've seen my mother in there. And then other times, completely sober, I've seen fire and death and well... all kinds of endings. Do you see that?

You'll notice that the frame barely does the thing justice. Eddie says he no longer wants the frame to upstage the beauty of the painting, and I can't entirely blame him because that isn't the same painting that hung on the wall when I moved in here. The original wasn't worth that much, truth be told. But the frame that used to house it was an heirloom and was worth a hell of a lot. I'm sure the burglar sold both for a fair price, and luckily they haven't been back since. I'm convinced there's some first editions over there on that bookshelf, and that's not taking into account the value of the jukebox and some of the vintage in the cellar. He liked the painting so much that he sought out a replica, but ultimately he blamed the theft on the frame and the sordid history of the pub. That new frame is nothing more than plywood. Shit, he's not even bothered to varnish the thing.

Did you happen to overhear anything about The Man in the Pinstripe Suit while you were ordering drinks? Nothing? I've never seen the guy here before, and the place basically survives on its carousel of regulars.

What's he drinking?

Whiskey.

No ice? So maybe he is Scottish.

Did you get a look at the guy's face? No. Not to worry, I'm sure his story will unravel after a few more of these. I guess we were both alone to begin with too, and it's not like either of us are here to cause trouble. Unless... no, I'm kidding! Really, I'm kidding. There's a comfortable familiarity about that second beer though, isn't there? It's like a homecoming! We'll toast to The Amsterdam and it's rich history, shall we?

Cheers.

It really has been a nice change to have a conversation with somebody about something other than landmarks and the weather. Truly, I thank you. Now, where were we? Ah yes, the worst thing I ever did. That'll require a few more gulps of this, if you don't mind.

I'll preface this with a little disclaimer. I've recently been through a period of upheaval, if you could call it that. I've moved around a lot, and it wasn't immediately clear to me what exactly I was searching for or when I'd stop. Maybe I haven't yet stopped completely, who knows? But before all of this... upheaval, are we agreeing to call it? Before that I was fairly settled in a more traditional way. I was born in Manchester, a city reborn amongst the Industrial Revolution into a kind of powerhouse of creativity and art. I guess a little of that rubbed off on me as I grew up, and I became interested in literature and music instead of football. I drew the same deep feeling of belonging from the written word and minor keys as many of my friends did from terrace chants and away days. Both have equal value, I must add, I just felt it was important to give you an insight into my upbringing for this story to have the desired effect. I've always been an over thinker, despite the extroverted nature of myself in public. You needn't look so worried, I'm not going to tell you my entire life story. And drink your beer! I know you're listening, I don't need your undivided attention. Please, relax.

Now, in my early twenties I managed to tick off a number of the traditional boxes. First, I used my degree to qualify as an English teacher, and found myself a comfortable job teaching small groups of willing college students about literature. An impossible job really for somebody so young, but I always felt that I had luck on my side. I quickly made a name for myself through what I guess was a combination of youthful enthusiasm and hard work. My students enjoyed my lectures and read much more widely than I ever did, teaching me more than I could hope to learn from books. In retrospect, I was luckily to hold their respect at such a young age. I remember distinctly the feeling of having everything figured out, as if a path had been cleared of weeds ahead of me. But reading so much literature had undoubtedly taken its toll on me. I had long been at the whim of my emotions, finding them to be a more natural guide than logic or forward planning, and there was always something missing. It became clear to me, only after meeting Simone, that I had finally found it. Simone taught philosophy in the same college. I was twenty five at the time we started our relationship, and she a full ten years older. Something about this took the pressure off, I think. Her effortless calm in the face of everything made it easier for her intellect to shine through.

She was so smart.

Smarter than maybe anyone I've met since. Her wisdom had this way of congealing inside her eyes - one of which was miraculously slightly bluer than the other - so that I would always know when she was on the verge of some great philosophical idea. I could have conversations with her that were much more interesting than years of conversations I had previously had with some of my lifelong friends. I used to watch her think, if you understand my meaning. Listen to the cogs turning inside her head. I'd watch and wait and hope that she would find the time to share something from her inner monologue with me. And when she did, well, she did so with just the slightest echo of her native French that... I digress.

What I am trying to tell you is that I was happy, fulfilled, and yes... I think I was in love. At least in the way it was described in books. I had everything figured out. My mother was proud of me. She told me that she always knew I was special, and that I was always destined for great things. "You're a good person, that's why" she would say. "Good people receive good things in return." And so I was convinced. My students reinforced this. They told me that no other teacher was able to explain Wilde in the way I did. No other teacher made the Romantics seem interesting. No other teacher would take hours out of their day to ensure the pupils in their class were getting along with each other, if they had enough money to get the bus home, or if everything had finally resolved itself with their on-again off-again sweetheart. They told me I was different, just like my mother did. And Simone? Well, she didn't have to. She was my reward for being a good person. Her smile and her slightly crooked front tooth were the result of my good karma. The fact that an older woman wanted to be with me in the first place was because I had led a good life and I was unlike every other twenty five year old in the city. I was the protagonist in everybody's story, not just my own, and I was hurtling towards a happy ending. I deserved it, you know?

THE HYPOCRITE

That's how I felt. I'm not some egomaniac who came here to gloat either, I just want you to understand how it felt to be me at that point in my life. I felt unstoppable.

But yes, you are right. That feeling is impossible to sustain. We are all controlled by countless unavoidable factors that seek to hinder us rather than help. Our emotions for one are combustible. We aren't built, as human beings, to exist in a world that cares about us so little. It doesn't have that ability because it simply is. The universe is an unpredictable sequence of cause and effect reactions, and all we can do is our best.

Later that year my mother died.

No, really, you don't have to apologise. It is terrible, but it happens to everyone eventually. I don't mind talking about it, actually. It happened at a difficult age, that's for sure. No, no, I don't mind answering that. She died suddenly, it was a complication with her surgery. The worst part about the whole thing, except losing her, was that it was a completely unnecessary procedure. Breast augmentation. Tummy tuck. That sort of cosmetic stuff. Yeah, really awful. Freak accident really. What angered me at the time was the reason she paid so much money to have such an invasive procedure.

I mean, we all care about how we are perceived, don't we? We all care about our looks, how attractive we are, how successful we appear. I guess it just got to her more than most.

The reason I'm telling you this, other than to reinforce my point that the universe is untameable and sometimes cruel, is a selfish one. I want you to understand why I did certain things, and how I ended up here in Edinburgh. I'd hate my decisions to seem rash or hyperbolic, because as I've just explained, we all care deeply about how we are perceived.

Even you, no?

That wasn't it, you see. The worst thing I ever did wasn't paying for her surgery - I didn't - or failing to tell her that I loved her. I did that as often as I got the chance. What I will say is that it's impossible to predict how the loss of somebody so integral to your life will affect you. I had lost my champion - the person who had always told me I was special and good. I came to doubt the things I had always thought of as absolute. With nobody to blame or attack, I directed my anger at the universe, and I confess I began to question what I had always believed to be true. The seed was planted then.

Why should I strive to be good if this is how I am rewarded?

I know that to be unhealthy. Dangerous almost. You felt similar things in the face of loss, you say? You're right, it's natural. But I guess you could say that I took her death personally. It seemed to attack everything I'd ever believed to be true, after all.

Sorry. I do tend to scratch when I get stressed or uncomfortable. It's eczema. It only really brothers the crooks of my arms these days but, well, it caused me some unease in my youth. I apologise, it's hardly good table manners but I assure you that it's all subconscious. Dare I say it's a little too warm in here now? Not that I'd fancy my chances against the tundra just yet.

Ah! A happy coincidence. Is that the book that's been sat on the table this whole time? Sometimes it's hard to argue that the universe is completely unpredictable, isn't it? Even after the conversation we've just had.

Choose Your Own Adventure - Journey Beneath The Ice. I remember these things. Eddie keeps a couple over there on the bookshelf. The last person to occupy this table must have needed a little escapism, eh? I enjoy the cover, don't you? The north pole, northern lights, is that... is that a flying saucer beneath the ice, there? Or the dome of some kind of long forgotten temple? Fun, but I fear they teach people the wrong lessons. How convenient would it be to be able to take back a decision you made by just turning back a couple of pages?

You've been eaten by shark... turn back to page seventeen.

The ice sheet collapses on top of you! No worries, I'll just go back a page.

The UFO activates its laser cannons and kills everyone you love! Turn back to page whatever. I'm being maudlin again, aren't I? You'll have to stop me sooner next time, I fear I'm becoming miserable.

Should we counteract that feeling by buying another drink? My round, of course. You see, that's cheered me up!

Turn to page forty-two to ask the Man in the Pinstripe Suit his name.

Turn to page thirty to buy a round of drinks.

Turn to page thirteen to explain the worst thing you ever did.

Let me grab those beers, and then I'll get into it.

I won't keep you in suspense any longer.

MOUNTAINEERING

So, the worst thing I ever did.

I was still recovering from losing my mother. That's not an excuse, I'm just saying that because it's true. The grief I expected. It's something that's common to human experience, and although it's profoundly horrible, it is manageable with a heavy dose of time and patience. I'd stopped mourning at this point as she'd been gone close to year. I'd blamed the surgeon, myself, my mother, her friends and colleagues even, but I always arrived at the same conclusion. It was a cruel twist of fate, and there was no escaping it. The idea of 'deserving' her destiny was far from the point. The idea of her being a good person was beside the point, too. I also found it difficult to avoid the selfish line of thought that her death had happened to me. It was that protagonist syndrome again.

Despite the creeping feeling that living life for any greater purpose was somehow futile and trivial, I did attempt to carry on. My teaching suffered, of course. I had once regarded literature as a weapon to be used to combat mortality. For the writer it was a way to endure and remain after death - they could contribute to society and conversation long after their physical body had decomposed. And for the reader, for my students and I, the written word was used to find meaning in a meaningless world. For a time you could say literature served me in the way faith in God serves so many others. Literature was transcendence.

Still, I wasn't myself and my students could see that. I looked tired. I made flippant remarks whilst teaching Stevenson's *The Strange Case of Dr Jekyll and Mr Hyde* about the merits of Mr Hyde, a cruel murderer and vagabond who was as far removed from being a 'good' person as it was possible to be. I'm still not sure if moving to Edinburgh was entirely a coincidence or something else I took from that man and his book. My students saw a change in me. They knew my ability to care was dwindling, and true to form, their opinions no longer mattered to me. But, despite this change in my worldview, I still wholeheartedly believed that I was a good person. The thing that had changed was the world's indifference to me - its failure to reward my good behaviour.

But then something happened that changed all of that.

I'd decided to move from Manchester to Edinburgh, just to have some time away from the little things that reminded me of Mum. It was a collection of stupid memories at first. Songs we'd sung along to in the car when I was little. Holidays. Falling asleep on her shoulder watching sentimental Sunday afternoon movies. But there was a kind of cumulative effect going on, and those memories went from being nostalgic to painful pretty quickly. The smell of a perfume even similar to hers in the high street made my stomach turn. I expected her to be behind every corner I turned or door I opened, and I was angry at her for it now, rather than just upset. I was dealing with some serious shit, you could say.

So I took a leave of absence from teaching and climbed from the bowels of Waverley station, dragging a suitcase on wheels. I liked how different it looked here. A city somehow caught between two periods of time that proudly wore its conflicting personalities on its lapel like enamel pins. I felt instantly inspired and yet I had no idea what I would do with my time. As soon as I'd set myself up I'd call Simone. We'd agreed, as sensible adults, to try the long distance thing. Besides, at this point I hadn't decided how long I was staying and really, how could she have known? It only dawned on me later that perhaps she already did know and it was me who was wading through the dark.

Stalling? That doesn't sound like me. I just don't want to let my beer go flat, that's all. And, well, I happened to notice that The Man in the Pinstripe Suit was talking rather angrily on his phone. Maybe you were right! Do you think he's been stood up? What language is that he's speaking? I don't think it's Russian. No, not Hungarian either. Somewhere in the region of-

- okay, I'm sorry. No more stalling. I promise.

It happened on a rare sunny day. It was one of those where it was quite frankly impossible to wallow or feel sorry for yourself, even in my situation. I'd been in Edinburgh close to a week but I could barely remember anything I'd done. There were buskers in the street playing the songs of the city's past, only in slightly more hopeful voice. The puddles had evaporated and for once nobody felt the need to wear a jacket. I myself was carrying a blazer under one arm, and I confess I was getting a little carried away with it all. Even if this is all futile, I remember thinking, there is nothing that can stop me enjoying this moment. This right now is actually quite nice, and maybe it doesn't have to mean anything. I thought, you know, that maybe it was time to take some of the pressure off. Maybe that's why

THE HYPOCRITE

I was feeling so rough.

This train of thought encouraged me to take a longer route home. In doing so the sunbeams fell on my face and worked their magical chemical reaction to the point that I'm sure I visibly smiled, unimpeded by thoughts of what the people passing by may have thought. And then I remembered that I'd never got round to conquering Arthur's Seat, the peak of a group of hills in the city's east that overlooked everything like a proud grandfather. It never looked too appealing in the rain when it's summit was hidden behind cloud, but today it puffed its chest out invitingly and I was suddenly in the mood. It was to be an entirely selfish walk, and one that I was sure I both needed and deserved. I smiled the entire way to Holyrood Park, enjoying leaving behind the sound of sirens, and therefore danger, in the city. Having not completed any research, I began my ascent up one of the more challenging routes wearing only Chelsea boots and a t-shirt. As a minimum requirement my fellow adventurers wore at least the correct footwear, but some added to that professional camera equipment or entirely unnecessary waterproof gear and walking aids. I rolled my eyes to entertain myself but didn't let my cynicism sully my mood. The sun and the seemingly filtered air spurred me on. There must have been something either inviting or ridiculous about me at this point in the climb, just as - have you been there yet? Well, the path I took kind of dips down into a valley. This huge bowl surrounded by crags and steep inclines on all sides. To my left was Arthur's Seat, and to my right, suddenly, was an American woman.

She made a joke about my shoes and I respected her for it. I deserved it, I felt. Particularly in the company of those who had made the effort. She reassured me by telling me I was young and probably fit, and then in possible reaction to my searching glances and unspoken worry, ran through her own credentials. She had climbed a few mountains back home in the US, all of which had much more sinister names like Rattlesnake Ridge or Tiger Mountain, and so I guessed she'd be fine. We synchronised our pace and Wendy filled me in on a few details of her own life. She had been divorced a number of years and had two children - one that hated her and another that was at best indifferent. Her current companion, Phil, refused to commit to anything romantic and yet was currently in her family home in Washington dog sitting as a favour. She had come to Edinburgh alone, just like me. And let me just say in hindsight, thank fuck she wasn't wearing any perfume that reminded me of Mum.

It seemed like we were both in a pretty bad place.

We reached an intersection in which you could start a fairly daunting climb up stone steps to the very summit, or climb a slight grassy ridge which took you to a sheer drop overlooking the city. Wendy was out of breath by this point and my boots were covered in mud, and so we both decided to take the easy option and look out from the nearest viewpoint. We were a team now. I tensed up as I watched a couple of children playing close to the edge because the horizon was playing a perspective trick which made the drop look much closer than it actually was.

I remember physically closing one eye in discomfort, like this.

Wendy told me she didn't mind heights, not anymore. She walked on a little but I was perfectly happy with the view and the distance I had created between myself and imminent doom. I took out my phone, thinking I'd send a photo to Simone and trying to suppress the memory of the other person I would ideally have sent it to. I closed both my eyes now, in some kind of pointless gesture that I hoped could somehow block out bad memories. Behind my eyes, and

I remember this as vividly as I do everything from this point onward, galaxies swam and coalesced much clearer than they had ever before. Some destroyed others and some destroyed themselves. When I opened my eyes I saw that Wendy had broken into a run.

It was clear to me that she had decided to join in with the children's game, whatever it was, but they had stopped laughing and were standing with their mouths agape quite some distance from their parent's and the safety of their picnic blanket. Wendy didn't stumble or hesitate. She put one foot in front of the other until there was no distance left to run, and disappeared silently over the edge of the cliff with a small, unimpressive leap.

I know what you're thinking. There was nothing I could have done to help her, right? I suppose, and I've thought about this a lot, there was nothing I could have done to stop her jumping. Even if I'd have been quicker to react, I probably wouldn't have reached her in time. But it was what I did afterwards that I think of as the worst thing I ever did, and the thing that destroyed almost everything I had known about myself and my place in the world from then on. I stared blankly at the view, my phone hanging listlessly at my side, and closed my eyes again. Somehow by doing this I think I hoped to erase the last thirty seconds of my existence. I've no idea how long I stood there with my eyes closed, or how to explain the cocktail of emotion that still shifted and changed within the pit of my stomach. I could swear that some of those emotions were new - not guilt or grief, but something entirely unmapped and unrecorded. Something different to what I was running away from. When I opened my eyes nothing had changed. I hadn't even checked to see if Wendy was still alive. Eventually a scream rose from somewhere beneath the crag and the atmosphere changed all at once. It felt like somebody had turned down the sunlight and turned up the dread. The children, inherently sensing that something was wrong but not knowing what it was, started to cry and sought the attention of their parents. People started to figure out what had happened, looking over the edge of the cliff with hands over their mouths or cupping their faces. There were tears and panic and phone calls. All the while I stood there and didn't move an inch.

And that was exactly the thing that destroyed me. I didn't know who I was anymore. I'd always thought of myself as a model citizen. In fact, I'd fantasised about situations just like this in the past. Rescuing children from burning buildings, pushing the elderly out of the way of speeding cars, single-handedly stopping a gunman in my local shop and having my picture framed on the wall like Eddie's Dad, over there. I saw television interviews, magazine covers and movie scripts based on my true story. But there I was, standing further than necessary from the edge of a cliff, frozen in inaction.

And it gets worse.

When I eventually found myself able to move, I didn't rush to help. I didn't tell anyone I'd met the woman, or that I had some idea of how unhappy she was. Christ, the last thing I wanted anybody to find out was that I had actually experienced a rush of guilt-tinged joy when Wendy had recounted the details of her sad life. I was relieved that somebody seemed to be more lost than I was, and nothing about me wanted to help her. I wasn't going to share my story because then she would have come out on top, and I'd have been the failure. So with these thoughts and regrets, I turned on the spot and retraced our steps back through the valley. I later found out that Wendy didn't survive her fall.

Arthur's Seat would have to wait.

BARSTOOL

I didn't say anything. I couldn't! People don't like to be interrupted, never mind by strangers. Besides, he's still on the phone. Less angry now, admittedly, but not altogether in a good mood. Eddie fired off a warning shot with his eyes, too, like he knew who he was. I guess we could just ask Eddie who he is after he leaves? Anyway, I've switched us to rum. I hope you like dark and stormy, but judging by the look on your face you approve anyway. It's my favourite drink, and I must confess I'm in need of something to take the edge off after my confession.

You're very kind. But you see, that was only the first in a series of deplorable things that coloured that part of my life. I knew I was going to stay in Edinburgh right from the moment of the fall, and yet I had nowhere near the courage to tell Simone. Right then the easiest thing to do was to keep my feelings hidden, to lie to her and to myself, and maybe that's why I now keep such an open book policy. It didn't do me any good, as you can imagine.

I descended the hill and retraced my footsteps through the park, getting out just in time for a police cordon to be assembled behind me. It felt symbolic in a way, that I was leaving it behind, but of course it wasn't. Things rarely are. I was alone in that moment and needed to be around people, if only to catch some of their positivity by osmosis. Despite me expressing my disinterest in conversation about the weather or work, that was exactly the kind of banal chat I hoped to be bathed in as soon as possible. Dangerously, for the first time in my life, I felt like I needed a drink rather than wanted one.

I didn't know The Amsterdam at that point, but even if I did I imagine I wouldn't have wanted to poison it with how I was feeling. It gets a little easier to explain here, actually. I remember feeling completely empty and more than a little scared. Probably what scriptwriters are going for when their characters say they feel 'numb' after a particularly traumatic experience. It was an amplified anxiety, like I was always in the middle of a game of hide and seek and could hear the sound of footsteps on the landing. I think part of me was worried I was going to be a suspect in a murder case, which I never was of course, or even that some kind of cosmic judgement would rain down on me because I still believed that was how the universe worked. For the first time in my life I felt like a coward and a fraud, but I didn't yet have the ability to revel in those emotions or make them work in my favour. Instead I ordered a whiskey despite not really having a taste for it. I wanted to punish myself, I think. It got late and - wow, this dark and stormy is really good, isn't it? - I sank a few more completely random drinks that I had probably seen depressed men drinking in movies. All whiskey based of course, like our man at the bar. Nothing that had connotations of happiness or reminded me of fonder times. No dark and stormy. At this point I didn't want to cheer myself up, I wanted to see how deep the well went.

The bar filled up and soon people were jostling for space and talking loudly. I managed to keep dominion over my bar stool and keep my need for the bathroom at bay. My reflection in the mirror behind the spirits was such a sad sight that I remember laughing quite loudly at the state I'd found myself in. The humour eventually gave way to anger, which was a feeling I was barely familiar with. It actually took me a few moments to compose myself enough to identify it. Then I really started homing in on people's conversations, and people, especially drunk people, talk about the most agonising things. A group of men in the corner projected their mundane and unoriginal sexual fantasies on a girl across the bar who was half their age. A larger group of women screeched loudly at regurgitated office jokes, desperately holding on to their group identities and playing to them for effect. 'The sexy one' winked at one of the leering men in the corner but he obviously felt far too superior to reciprocate. Soon he was telling one of his comrades that he'd fuck her if he could put her head in a paper bag. A couple standing at the bar rubbed their happiness in everyone's faces but especially mine. To add insult to injury, an obnoxious prick showed off his new watch and spoke in an offensively southern accent about how much he paid for it. Unfortunately for this man, he was standing just a little bit too close to my barstool for my liking.

Have you ever been in a fight?

I honestly believe that everyone should get punched in the face once in their life. It's humbling. However, I never had the joy of actually landing a punch so maybe that's where that misguided philosophy comes from. Who knows. Long story short, I tried in vain to land a punch on this guy's face, thinking I'd follow it up with some kind of clever one-liner like "time's up, pal" or "don't tick me off". But not only could I not find a decent pun, my punch was embarrassingly off target and just weak enough to land in the guy's lap like a dead fish. Worst of all, the guy wasn't as obnoxious as I first thought. He was shocked, yes, but he actually helped me to my feet and told me to calm down instead of knocking me to the ground like I deserved. There was genuine pity in his eyes. So I swing again, this time nearly hitting one of the girls in his company and feeling more like scum than ever but revelling in it. Firmly this time, but on reflection only with necessary force, my target effortlessly wrestled me into a headlock, and before I knew I was falling backwards I had made contact with the Royal Mile.

You're right to look at me like that. If that was a Choose Your Own Adventure book you'd immediately know you'd turned to the wrong page and were heading for one of the more ambitious, sad endings. But you must understand where I was coming from. The fact that the man with the watch didn't rise to my attack only reflected what I used to be, a good-natured citizen of the world. For all I knew he deserved that watch and the beautiful girl I had made cry with my recklessness. The universe was not only failing to reward me, it was now, as I saw it, actively punishing me for what happened beneath Arthur's Seat.

If you're driving a car on ice and lose control, people wiser than you tell you to steer into the skid against all your better judgement. So over the next few days I took their advice. I paid twenty pounds for a ghost walk around the city, but got kicked off half way through for being drunk and calling bullshit on everything the thoroughly Scottish guide had to say. I told him and whoever else would listen that life was pointless and so the very idea of an afterlife was even more ridiculous than he already knew. And he did know. You could see in his eyes that he knew, but the poor man was only trying to make a living and barely anyone had turned up. I think that's why he let me stay for so long.

I'd already started to ignore Simone because I felt I was no longer good enough for her. She'd initially given me space, as we'd agreed, but over the course of the last few days she'd begun bridging the gap. A few messages at first, telling me she was worried about me, that she hoped I was okay, and explaining the details of some academic journal she was contributing to so I didn't suspect she was having an affair. Of course I felt that the academic journal part was overkill and that she was definitely seeing somebody more age appropriate and less damaged behind my back. I also wondered for the first time if the students I had taught for so long missed me, or if they too had been gifted an improved model. You'll be able to tell by the tone of this part of the story where my head went for an answer to that.

You're right to laugh. I'd gotten myself in quite a state, actually. I was living in a hostel on a permanent basis with a Portuguese man who worked nights in a factory. He'd been there six months and as his sad eyes would attest that was nothing to aspire to. But it was a semi-permanent place to hide from my real life and I was starting to enjoy Edinburgh for what it had become - a place for me to wallow and not attract unnecessary attention. I disappeared from Simone's life without so much as an explanation after that. Even if you take away the self-loathing, I just thought it'd be much easier to be on my own for a while, even if I did probably love her.

I went on like this for a while, constantly choosing the wrong adventure. Flicking to pages where my life took the wrong turn and wondering why I wasn't being reprimanded. I wasn't looking after myself and my eczema, I think I mentioned it earlier, returned from my childhood to blight me. It's easy to think of it as some aesthetic thing - to boil it down to dried out skin and scratching, but it was a lot worse than that. It affected my self-confidence, sure, having inflamed red sores on your face will do that to anybody. But then I stopped being able to sleep, and when I eventually did I'd subconsciously attack myself and wake up covered in scratches in a blood-stained bed. I could neither cool down nor concentrate. At its worst I was embarrassed to go out in public unless I was fully covered up, and so I slept most of the day and only went out at night to drink and be around people when it was less obvious. The alcohol made it worse, of course, but it seemed then to be the antidote to loneliness. It might as well have said it on the bottle.

No I don't think we're being hypocritical, not really. Or if we are, at least we've called it out. I've certainly done a lot that could fall into that category, but drinking sociably is something I've regained my ability to do. I must be depressing the hell out of you, no? Again, you're too kind for letting me vent like this. I've learned a lot, and maybe you'll find something to take away from my story that will help you.

Maybe you'll make your own mistakes, or maybe you'll turn to the right page and continue down a better path. Personally, I decided to stay in Edinburgh and obviously I'm still here. I had a lot of rebuilding to do, I know that, but at least now I know I was right to come here and I'm content with my place in the world.

How many people can truly say that?

Hey - it looks like our guy in the suit has decided to stay a little while longer. I wonder if he's feeling the same way I did after coming down from the mountain? And there goes his jacket, if he's not careful he's going to drop-

- did you hear that? What the hell has he got in the inside pocket to make a noise like that as it hits the floor? Oh, and look! He's apologising. He's apologising and he's worried that he's drawn attention to himself. That's something important - why else would he be frantically checking it like that? I wish he'd let us see. Damn. What are you thinking? A handgun? Ha! I'm sure it'll be less sinister than that. An engagement ring perhaps? A secondary phone? God I'll be disappointed if we never find out. I'm far too invested.

Another drink?

MEZZANINE

Please don't tell me he's leaving... He's putting his jacket back on but I guess it is below freezing out there. I think... I think he's just going out for a cigarette. You're right - if he doesn't come back we can just ask Eddie. Okay, okay - keep your voice down he's passing right by us. Don't make it obvious. I *said* don't make it - he's gone. He's gone but hopefully not for good. Anyway, I found something to keep us busy until he comes back on my way back from the bar... Two more!

Escape From The Tomb of Horus, which even my rudimentary knowledge of Egyptology tells me is a load of shit, and *The Mystery Beneath The Mountain* which looks so sinister I'm a little worried about all the children that read it by accident. I mean... look at that picture! Is it a demon or is it supposed to just flat out be the devil? I suppose if I were to be a little more positive about these Choose Your Own Adventure books as a genre, they at least teach kids that they have the power to make decisions. The power to change things.

It says here that the writer had to plot out huge, sprawling outlines to make sure all the timelines fitted together and could co-exist in the same book. Here, I'll read it to you when it loads up.

Come on…

Okay, here we go. He describes the outlines as 'like a tree lying on its side with many branches and limbs' which I imagine is just like a flowchart but this was probably said before computers or something. It's interesting, though, don't you think? Are there just infinite versions of us, running around failing or succeeding in reaction to every choice that's made? What if I'd asked The Man in the Pinstripe Suit his name already? Or not engaged you in conversation, for example?

Things like that really get me going.

I think that's because I've always felt I make a lot of choices. Or at least I'm always aware of how catastrophic they might be as I'm making them. The most interesting choices are the ones you don't feel like you're making at all, those that seem to happen no matter how much you ignore, avoid or intervene. Some people call those things destiny, don't they? It's like ending up in the snake pit on page forty-two of *Escape From The Tomb of Horus*, no matter how careful you were not to be followed through Cairo, or how many traps you deactivated on the way in. Some things just happen and there's nothing we can do about it.

This was the school of thought I managed to buy into maybe a month after the accident at Arthur's Seat. I couldn't blame myself for the way I acted or the way I felt, and I decided that I had learned a lot from that afternoon. I decided I was destined to be there, and that it was part of the process I needed to recover from whatever it was I was trying to recover from. As fate would have it, just as I was running out of money a job came up in the box office of King's Theatre. I was merely knocking on the door of drunk when I saw the flyer in the window, and so had the good sense to take a picture of the vacancy and apply the next day when my head was a little clearer. When the day came to interview I stepped into my old teaching suit and blagged a love of the arts and the plays I had taught as a literature teacher. Cleverly, I left out my recent alcoholism and brushings with suicide. My biggest fear at this point was that the theatre was somehow affiliated with the men who conducted ghost walks, and that they had seen my mugshot on some kind of wanted list. Thankfully my misdeeds were never mentioned and I was welcomed with open arms.

Time is a great healer, but for the impatient, friendship and belonging are just as good. For the first time in a great deal I began to feel like I could claw back something of the life I had left behind in Manchester, and the people I met at the theatre were the reason for that. When they looked at me they didn't see Arthur's Seat or my mother or Simone. They simply saw a man with a funny accent who was willing to dive headfirst into any given opportunity. I stayed late, cracked jokes, gave the regulars nicknames and was given my own in return.

The King's started to become the place I felt the most at home, wearing my mask of art and leaning into the 'man with a secret history' angle I'd accidentally created. I ended up being able to drink with a fantastic circle of beautiful people. Most of these were steeped in false ambition, clinging onto sub-par roles and relying on the annual Fringe Festival for structure and purpose. Others were just delaying the real world, along for the ride and nothing more. You know the type. It was like Hollywood in the thirties only it never really got off the ground and was much colder. Oh sure, some did have real talent, but I like to focus on the underdogs. Which leads me to Steinbeck.

Steinbeck, formally known as Robert McInerney, was bestowed with his nickname because he used to write a lot and had a penchant for grapes, which he called 'nature's sweets' without irony. He was part of the acting ensemble up at The Kings and we got to talking and drinking and telling stories. Although I didn't see the fun in telling him everything, we got to know each other well enough to rent a place above a Cat Cafe in New Town.

Oh no, the Cafe was for people. The cats were just heavily featured.

You purchase drinks and spend time with the resident cats, who are forced to spend their lives with an endless rotation of replaceable faces. They seem happy enough there, but I have always wondered how they get these places licensed. Steinbeck would leave food on our balcony and the cats would come up to us 'for a break from work', as he described it. The cat hair was terrible for my eczema, sure, but I appreciated the company too much to allow myself to reach that conclusion.

Soon I was feeling much more like myself, whoever that was, and the shaky start to my time in Edinburgh was starting to break up and dissolve into memory. Steinbeck encouraged me to write, which became another thing for me to monologue to - the cats being the first. I wrote songs and poems at first, but did start and abandon a number of screenplays. Embarrassing stuff really, just my own spin on things that have already been said. They never felt worth it. I began to feel like I needed instant gratification for my 'art', as I was already calling it, and Steinbeck and I fell into a period of self-importance. After all, this was a replacement for my friends, family and career. I decided I might as well do it properly.

None of us could remember why we'd called the band Mezzanine. I was the singer because I couldn't play an instrument and enjoyed the feeling of sitting up at night writing out lyrics and making shitty recordings on my phone to show Steinbeck, who played guitar. Another actor we knew, Kevin, joined on bass and an actress I got to know quite well called Owen-

- Oh, no need to apologise. Simply O, W, E, N.

Ac*tress*, yes.

She made everything better.

The drums were the best bit of Mezzanine and Owen soon became my favourite part of Scotland. Her unpredictability was the thing that attracted me to her, the thing that made us argue and the thing that made me stay. She'd go full method when researching a part, even if that meant I had to hang around with a forty year-old man for a couple of days or sleep with a pensioner. And before you ask yes that did happen, and no, it wasn't as bad as you'd think. Owen was ambitious, and as I mentioned before, she was one of the small minority of people who did have genuine talent. Her acting moved me to tears on more than one occasion, although I'm still yet to work out if that was because I knew deep down that she would eventually be taken away from me.

I knew then what it felt like to be a cat in a Cat Cafe, if you'll excuse that horribly obvious analogy, and I started putting out expensive food on the balcony even when Steinbeck was away.

My skin got worse but my writing got better. Most importantly, I felt like I'd found people to champion me again. The cats gave me their undivided attention in return for fish-flavoured gloop. Owen encouraged me to sing and write down how I was feeling, as long as it rhymed and wasn't ripping off anyone she liked or thought I was trying to be. Steinbeck and Kevin found me interesting and weren't embarrassed to play behind me even when real bands were on the bill before and after us.

THE HYPOCRITE

I'd found meaning again. I was suspicious about the fleeting nature of the relationships I'd formed but I knew that art and music couldn't leave me and weren't frightened off by my fluctuating mood. If anything they thrived on it, and some days it was better to be in a bad mood than be in a good one. I stood at the back of Wendy's funeral and wrote a thinly-veiled song about it that afternoon. One of my screenplays clicked when I'd argued with Owen about why she had been missing for two days and why she was pretending to be an American lawyer. She even helped to read through it, playing the part based on herself and either not putting things together or proving her worth as an actress once again. I never wrote anything about Mum.

But that was the start of my recovery, friend.

Things were looking up. Edinburgh was home and my new family only knew what I wanted them to know about me. But there was still lot left to change, it was just I couldn't see it at the time. The second worse thing I ever did happened soon after Mezzanine, and I'm going to need another drink to dredge it up.

A couple more, perhaps? And look - hurrah! - The Man in the Pinstripe Suit has returned and smells, as predicted, like an ashtray. There is still time. But you're right, Eddie doesn't seem too pleased to see him does he? Even if he has already poured the man a drink.

I'll be right back.

HERO

Is he looking over because we were looking at him, or have we just caught him out? I hate that - the eye contact. It could have just been an accident that our eyes met but now it looks like we've been staring at him. Or, more confusingly, he's sitting over there in his suit thinking the exact same thing. I hope he doesn't come over. He does look like the type, doesn't he?

You're right. We're just sitting here having a nice time, minding our own business. I'll continue with the story you've been so patiently listening to in the hope that we forget about our friend over there. He's Eddie's problem.

Where was I? Oh yes, a rare moment of levity in the Edinburgh saga. I'd started feeling myself again, started believing my own mythos. And I think deep down I was aiming to prove it to myself once and for all. Undoubtedly and empirically, this time. I wanted confirmation that I deserved to be happy. That everything had happened for a reason. There was still this nagging doubt hiding in the corners, and although it's impossible to prove, I certainly felt like it was more prominent in me than it was in others. Nobody else seemed quite as self-aware as I felt, and they seemed all the better or it.

Things were going really well at The King's. Owen and I were in that irreplicable stage of a relationship that causes so much doubt and tension later on, and so we made an unspoken pact to enjoy it while it lasted. She stayed at mine as often as she could, and we'd read screenplays together instead of watching TV, challenging ourselves to play against type and resisting the urge to tease each other in order to bring out our most honest interpretations. That sounds pretentious, doesn't it? But that's where we were. We were amongst the pet names and the baby speak, reliving a part of our teenage years we'd never actually lived in in the first place. We'd joke sometimes about how by meeting we'd created an alternate timeline, and that within it nothing could go wrong. We'd both go on creating things and sheltering from the cold together until… well. Until we no longer did. Until one of us got sucked into the wrong timeline, I guess.

She's in London now, I think. Acting. I only ever see her at her happiest because of that trick that photographs play, but I do hope she has met a stranger in a similar, probably more expensive, bar in the capital and told them a version of our story. I wonder if she still

THE HYPOCRITE

remembers reading Vertigo as Jimmy Stewart?

Of course, my Kim Novak was just as convincing. I digress, as you'll no doubt remember me doing before my last confession. I'd ask where we were but I'd be being facetious.

Yes, things were going well. Steinbeck had written a particularly good play and was putting it into production at The King's, and so my main two companions were Owen and Jekyll, an off-white cat from downstairs. This was Edinburgh after all, and it's literary heritage was to be kept alive even by owners of possibly unlicensed novelty cafes. I told him stories through itchy eyes and wrote songs for Mezzanine between shifts on the box office and happier times with Owen. I scratched troughs into my arms and covered them up with long-sleeved shirts.

One Thursday after Jekyll had inevitably lost interest in me I took a walk over to Old Town to enjoy Edinburgh's prized drizzle and secondhand conversation. I caught the punchline of several contextless chats and smiled to myself, avoiding, as always, glancing at Arthur's Seat like the rest of the tourists. I walked past a memorably smug couple. A number of theories ran through my head that day as to its source, but nothing seemed obvious enough. As it turned out, simply walking in the opposite direction to me was one of the best decisions they ever made, and their smugness was justified.

So I climbed the stone steps onto the Royal Mile as I usually did. I pulled out my phone to catch a breather and to write down something I heard someone say because I thought it'd make a good lyric, but heard something horribly familiar to my right. It was a sound we'd all become accustomed to hearing through speakers - transmitted and transmuted - made into something less frightening by sheer distance and improbability. And then there was ducking and screaming and panicking.

And then someone had been shot.

And then somebody else, too.

You'll remember, no doubt. I can see in your face you remember. The gunman on the Royal Mile. The suspected Jihadi that transformed, with the absence of furore, into a psychopath homegrown in Scotland. News outlets began feeding for scraps almost immediately in the broken first-hand reports, in the 'eyewitness' accounts and the clues hidden in understandably shaky handheld footage. Now, I'm not sure if you'll entirely believe what I'm going to tell you next but I assure you I relive that afternoon every fucking night when I close my eyes and I'm telling the goddamned truth. A woman was shot multiple times right in front of me. Meters, if that. It's impossible, even now, to understand how fast time was moving. It's not impossible for me to understand, given the distance I've had, why I thought the woman that hit the cobbles was Wendy and why I thought I had time to save her. Why I thought I was capable of saving her. Why I thought that in the face of almost-certain death I'd run through a storm of shrapnel and throw myself over the body of a stranger. In that moment I was running down the bank of Arthur's Seat towards Wendy, calling for help and dialling the emergency services like an unbroken citizen and altering the course of my future. I'd turned back a couple of pages and was heading for a more satisfying and family friendly ending.

But of course I was just stood there, wide open, frozen to the spot with fear.

The situation escalated as my.... inaction, remained constant. Blood on the cobbles. Gun smoke in the air. Edinburgh Castle screaming internally in the background. And there was me, somewhere amongst the chaos, a useless observer once again. I'd seen my image on the front page of newspapers my entire life - Mum told me I was special, remember? - so I frequently put myself in imaginary peril and wondered just how I would prove myself to be the altruistic hero I'd promised myself I'd become. The one the prophecies foretold. As a kid I'd rehearsed my appearances on American chat shows, the jokes I'd tell on panel shows and even thought about how I'd structure my autobiography to ensure it became a cult classic.

This wasn't even my first chance at the title. This was my chance for redemption and yet there I was, pissing it into the breeze. I felt then, as I turned my back on a dying woman for the second time, the true futility of existence.

I'm really glad we decided on another drink. Damn. This got heavy again pretty quickly, didn't it? But there's absolutely no point in just showing you a reel of highlights. I hope by this point in the night that you understand how necessary it is that I finish my story.

I'm curious to know what you'll take from it. That's a good question, and one that I'm not afraid to answer. I hid down a side street until the bullets stopped and the wet cobbles were blue with the reflections of sirens. I was too humiliated to speak to any of the emergency services, and at that point if I'd been shot I believe I would have deserved it. I didn't go to work that day and I didn't go home. I sat in a franchise coffee shop until I got kicked out for not ordering anything, and then I wandered aimlessly until I heard of an impromptu vigil that was being held in Princes Street Gardens for the dead. Fifteen people, at that point. You'll remember it climbed to twenty-two the following day.

So I descended more stone steps and joined the secular congregation in lighting candles and singing Scottish songs I didn't know the words to. I remember just being around people felt like I was doing something, but of course I couldn't forget her. I couldn't forget Wendy or the woman on the cobbles and I couldn't forget what I had failed to do. Suddenly, you know, I'm crying and this older gentlemen has put his arm around me and he's saying 'there's nothing we could have done' and I'm just sobbing and telling him that there fucking was something I could have done and calling him a liar.

I remember him smelling like aniseed. But I wasn't crying because I was mourning or because the whole thing was inherently sad. The worst part is that I was crying for myself, because it felt good. I was crying because I knew once and for all that nothing I did mattered. I wouldn't be punished by the universe for not helping the dying women because the universe was entirely indifferent to the fact that I existed in the first place. Just like it was indifferent to my Mum. Just like it's indifferent to you.

Now, we're about to reach another fork in the road. I still had some entirely horrible things to accomplish that day, and I hope you won't judge me on them too harshly until you've heard my entire confession. I'll begin by saying that I can barely remember the rest of that day due to being drunk, but I want you to see that as a detail rather than an excuse.

I awoke in an atmosphere of regret. I'd shifted timelines, somehow. Without even opening my eyes I knew that things had irrevocably changed, I just couldn't quite bring myself to admit it. The alcohol and stress had made me scratch in the night, and parts of my skin burned and stung whilst my imagination painted a picture of the bloodied bedsheets. There was a stranger asleep next to me, a detail I had identified purely on their unfamiliar smell. Her unfamiliar smell. I tried to ignore reality in favour of a dream, but it didn't take.

Eventually I sat up and surveyed the scene. I was still wearing a condom, although it hadn't served its purpose and I hadn't fully served mine. I took it off and threw it in the bin, glancing at the sleeping girl in my bed and making a note of the constellation of spots around her chin. Even in her sleep she looked somehow on edge. It goes without saying that I had no idea who she was.

I took a naked walk into the living room and noticed Steinbeck's room was completely empty. There was a twinge in the corner of my memory like someone yanking on a thread. The only thing left in his room was a small handwritten note that said:

"I never had you down as the jealous type.

Get help.

Robert."

It still kills me that he used his real name, even now. It took me a long time to fully remember what I'd done, but he eventually told me the last time I spoke to him over the phone. I'd ruined the opening night of his play by turning up drunk and starting a fight with a man in the front row. Oh, I know. It gets worse - the lead was injured breaking things up and he had to postpone everything he'd worked so hard on. When I read through the messages I'd sent that night it turned out that I sent him some ideas about how to make the next draft better, including writing me into the second act. He read them, I think.

After I read the note I realised that my nose was pretty severely broken, and whilst I was fondling it I noticed another note in the kitchen, this time from Owen. I can remember that word for word, too. It said:

"Yesterday was the worst day of my life so far.

Enjoy your whore. Never contact me again.

P.S - Your Kim Novak impression was the most

embarrassing thing I've ever heard"

No, she didn't really write the last line, I just wanted to make you laugh. I suppose I'm deflecting again, aren't I, but things had taken a depressing turn. I dealt with things in worse ways back then, but humour isn't nearly as dangerous.

Safe to say I jumped right back into bed with that girl without knowing her name.

I wanted her to realise my nose was broken, or somehow understand that I was using her in the most abhorrent of ways, but she didn't. She pushed back against me with her eyes closed and made me feel like the scummiest man on earth. And really, who was going to tell me I wasn't?

LOOPHOLE

Don't make it obvious, but if you look over my left shoulder you'll see that our man is starting to act even stranger than before. I'll keep facing you and sipping my drink, but try to get a read on what he's up to. He's definitely not waiting for anybody, I think we can be sure of that now.

A cigarette? In here? I... Oh, I can hear Eddie. Jesus, was he really trying to light one up inside the bar? I know it looks a little underground here but come on, Eddie isn't going to allow that. How does he look? A little exasperated is a good thing. Much better than panic. They've not had proper security in here since I've been coming - I think Eddie's Dad was the last guy who held that post. I can hear talking... can you make out what they're saying?

The local news. Not a football fan, obviously. Bit rude to ask for the channel to be changed though, surely. I don't think I'd have the guts to ask in a bar I'd never been in before. Unless, well. Unless he has. As long as he's not looking over anymore I think we're safe to carry on with our drinks, although I have to admit I'm growing more and more curious about our man over there. I'll keep my eye on

Eddie. So, I pose a question: Is it worse to brag or to lie? I've never been sure. I suppose it depends on the situation, really. The reason I bring it up is because I don't want you to think I'm doing any of those things as I explain what happened to me after, well, everything.

Both are ugly. I'll tell you the truth if you'll listen, and I want you to frame those truths with this disclaimer: I am in no way proud of what I did in the months following Owen, Steinbeck and Mezzanine. The place I visited was reprehensible - I probably wouldn't go back - but it was a place I needed to visit so that I could get here, sharing a drink with you in The Amsterdam.

I hung around for a while in the flat after everyone left, my companions being my own filth and the frequent feline visitors from downstairs who came to rummage through the bins. The sink was out of action and I had no intention of wading through the shit that clung to the dishes to fix it. The light in the kitchen went. The indestructible houseplants died. My bedroom floor existed somewhere beneath socks, cutlery, dishes, books I was pretending to read, tissues and old tubes of steroid cream that were supposed to cure my eczema. I remember wanting Steinbeck or Owen to return quite badly, and the scene I had lovingly created in the flat above the

Cat Cafe was almost entirely for them. How were they supposed to feel sorry for me if they couldn't see what a state I was in? How were they supposed to forgive me?

But of course, that was the problem. I didn't want to apologise - I wanted an excuse. Like I said, I was in a bad place. Either Jekyll got sick of visiting or something in the great swathes of rubbish poisoned him, but I never had the guts to go downstairs to check. The owners hated me anyway. Besides, another cat had started to visit and I only had time for those who could accept me at my worst. This cat was entirely black and quite skinny, with a habit of swallowing the hair balls it had just coughed up. A masochist, just like me. I knew - mostly because of the collar I quickly disposed of - that the cat wasn't called Hyde, but I thoroughly enjoyed the symmetry in that narrative and decided that not only had this cat always been called Hyde, but that it had been sent to help me wallow.

So I kept him.

We hung out together for a while up there above the Royal Mile where the world media still circled for scraps of misery. There were lots more memorial services, charity singles and celebrity-fronted commiserations over those months, but I had become mostly immune to pain, or so I told myself. Nothing could hurt me, and even if it did it couldn't hurt more than what I'd already been through. I'd been one of life's nice guys up until that point, an upstanding citizen, somebody who contributed to society rather than one who fed off it. A giver rather than a taker. But it hadn't worked, and if something isn't working then the sensible thing to do is to adapt, isn't it?

And so I consciously became a dickhead. I lost my job at The King's because I didn't want to go back there after everything that had happened, and so my first task was signing on and collecting my welldeserved sixty pounds a week to spend on whatever my heart desired. I didn't say thank you to the faceless man that put my application through, nor did I apologise to the woman holding a coffee I barged past in the doorway on my way out. She called after me in a thick Scottish accent but the barbs just spurred me on, and I remember not even putting my hood up as I smiled and walked into the rain. I was my own evil twin and it felt fantastic.

I stole cat food for Hyde from a local shop on the corner of my road. I had absolutely no intention of paying my rent and knew that I would have to flee soon - but as Steinbeck was still an upstanding member of society he would undoubtedly deal with the landlord and foot the bill. Nice guys finish last, remember? With my days already numbered the only thing left to do was distract myself from impending doom. I began getting up later in the day and staying out later at night, ambling around student nights and taking amphetamines so that I could briefly feel unfiltered joy without immediate consequence. Life became a kind of game in which I was always trying to stop something from happening - whether that was sorting the flat out, calling people back or dealing with my hangover-slash-comedown in a realistic way. But there were always much easier alternatives, and in Edinburgh there was always something distracting and hedonistic to become embroiled in.

Soon I was getting kicked out of a stand-up shows for falling asleep on the front row, or this one time after heckling somebody in the most obnoxious way I could muster. There was this pub crawl from one of the hostels that stuck to a preordained route and I'd wait for them at one of the bars - sometimes O'Malley's or this shitty 'tiki bar' beneath the castle, and I'd be charming and wait for somebody to ask me to come along. I'd make friends for the night that made me feel like a real person, but my aim was to meet girls. It doesn't feel good to admit that, but that's where I was. The real breakthrough in my worldview was the discovery that I wasn't being punished for any of this behaviour. In the same way that I felt I was never rewarded for being a good person, I wasn't being punished by some external force for playing the villain. Things just kept happening as they always did. One thing after another thing. Unaffected by something as small and as pointless as me. And that wasn't as depressing as it sounds, I promise. It was liberating.

The girls I met at that time all blur into one, just as the lies I told them do. I'd tell them that they were different from the others, that I'd never met someone with their accent before, or that I also loved that film that they saw the day earlier. I'd tell them that I loved their laugh, their hair, or the way that only one dimple would appear in their cheek when they really laughed. I'd tell them that I lived just around the corner, and that there was really very little point in paying six pounds each for drinks when I had plenty in the flat. I'd say that I was actually going through a bit of a dry spell at the moment and that it was such a relief to meet somebody who could make me laugh or who could dance like they were the only person in the room. I'd pretend that the music was too loud for me to properly hear what they were saying in an effort to lead them outside and away from their rightfully suspicious friends. There's no point in paying for a taxi at this time. I feel like I've known you for years. I don't do this very often either.

There were consequences, but without guilt they were hollow and ineffective. There were some awkward mornings and forgotten names. I stopped being able to enjoy myself without a drink or a small bag of some not-quite-rare-enough chemical, which of course was the cheaper option if done properly. The cycle of night and day stopped being an accurate way to measure my actions, and I'd find myself out of control as I watched people heading to work or thoroughly lonely in the middle of the night. I'd look to Hyde for company and then spend the rest of the evening scratching myself because my sheets were covered in cat hair. Regardless of if it was socially acceptable or not, I'd soon find another misadventure to cling to just to get out of the house. It was around this time that I started visiting a sexual health clinic - not by choice of course, but just like the shoal of sad men under the fluorescent lights, because I had no other choice. I understand how this could seem like an unnecessary detail, by the way, but it's important as it explains how I met Dr. Kapoor - a man who just by listening helped me through whatever it was I was going through. Something about lying on a reclining plastic chair with my pants around my ankles stopped me from distancing myself too much or showing off, and so the appointments became strange, free counselling sessions. It was the first time I'd thought about teaching for a long time, and I enjoyed how impressed he seemed when I told him what I used to do for a living. Of course I told him I was still a teacher because I wasn't really anything anymore. His professional probes into my sex life led nicely into anecdotes that he seemed happy to listen to, and from my second and third visits we would ponder everything from philosophy and the human condition to his ranking of Woody Allen movies. He told me about his father being a freedom fighter of sorts in India, and I shared with him some insights about my own family and why I'd moved to Scotland in the first place. There were at least two occasions in which I had to stop myself from crying.

When I needed no further treatment I did consider taking a less careful approach to contraception in the hope that I could be reunited with my spirit guide and counsellor, but had no such luck. I made a note of his email address just in case I really found myself at a

THE HYPOCRITE

loose end and again flung myself into the abyss. Tyler, a thoroughly boring coding student who worked with the cats downstairs between library visits, sold me something that would help me remember why chatting to strangers through laserbeams and dry ice was worth my time.

A horrible side-effect of Tyler's concoction was that it convinced me that absolute strangers were old friends. It was an unnerving detail, but I'd sometimes see old teachers, family members and ex-girlfriends in rooms they weren't actually in. This is probably as interesting as talking about my dreams, I'm sure, but I need you to believe that when I say I was convinced Dr. Kapoor was there in that basement with me that you get a sense of how much I believed it. He was the only familiar face that didn't feel like an old friend - he was judgement personified. I'd lose sight of him for a while but then catch him sitting on a chair in the corner or holding my head with both hands and asking me if I was okay and if I wanted a glass of water. He was in every bathroom mirror, and the conversations he was having were always much louder than those of the other guests because he was always near, somehow. Always looking at me like he had under the lamp above the reclining plastic chair.

I found out then that Dr. Kapoor had actually been dead for thirty years.

Just kidding, obviously.

But it freaked me out, for sure. I felt judged, finally. So the next day I didn't go to any parties. I stayed in bed. Eventually I fell asleep and woke up the next day, amongst the bad memories and the cat I loved but was horribly allergic to. We made the decision to leave around that time, and because I had no money I asked Simone to lend me some money so that I could get out of Edinburgh for a while. I even asked her to come, knowing that there was no way she wasn't better off without me. She knew how hard it must have been for me to get into contact, I think, and that's why she helped me out. I can't tell you how nice it was to hear from her, someone from my original timeline, before I'd started choosing the wrong adventures. She didn't want an explanation, and so I offered her an apology instead. I remember that making me smile as I stood there in the dark with my phone wedged between my ear and my shoulder because I knew where I had to go. I can't remember if I was crying or not.

Which reminds me.

THE HYPOCRITE

This book here. The one we we've been looking at. I happen to know a little about these Choose Your Own Adventure things because I've spent so much time here alone. Telling you about that regrettable part of my life has reminded me of how difficult these books could be to win. You see, once the general public had accepted the concept of multiple endings the author found they were becoming a little too formulaic - you'll see that if you rifle through a couple of them - and so he started adding more endings and more possibilities. But when that didn't satisfy his creativity he created something else. A loophole, if you will. He began to hide secret endings in his adventures, but none of the pages could lead you there. They existed in isolation, in another timeline entirely from the logical stories he laid out in his plans.

That's precisely the question I wanted you to ask! The only way to get to the secret ending was to turn to the wrong page.

You could only reach it by accident.

BEACH

With Simone's help I took a little time out. Whatever feeling of disconnect I had experienced in Manchester was now creeping in over the border, and I wanted to get out before everything got infected.

There were a few things I took care of before I left, even though I knew I'd return in a few days. I always liked working to a deadline and so the idea of having a clean break from Steinbeck's place - moving out with the intention of never moving back in - gave me the illusion that my life had some kind of forward momentum. I sent Dr. Kapoor an anonymous email despite knowing that my name appeared in some form in my email address, letting him know that he had no idea how much he had helped me even if we were to forget about my genitals, which I sincerely hoped he had. I thought about contacting Owen or Steinbeck but instead left a dramatic handwritten note in the flat that I knew nobody would ever read. I won't bother telling you what it said - I'm sure you can imagine at this point. But the one thing I'm a little proud of was a letter - yes, handwritten - that I sent Simone thanking her for forgiving me and giving me the resources I needed for my second fresh start. I managed to put my ego to one side for the briefest of moments, so I hope you'll forgive me this small brag. If only to make myself feel better. A train and a bus took me to Pease Bay, this charming little cove on the west coast of Scotland. You should check it out, it isn't far from here. I checked into Hotel Dakota, which was within spitting distance of the Atlantic, and sat in the lap of one of its huge stone windows. There was a mesh between my alcove and the sea that prevented seagulls from roosting there, and yet still they circled, as if one day their luck would change and they would have access to the finest real estate in Scotland. The feeling I had then was remarkably similar to when I first emerged from Waverley Station and took in the castle the day I moved to Edinburgh - this irreplicable freedom edged with a tangible excitement. There was a melancholy there too, but one I rather liked and felt necessary. I didn't try very hard to find a shop as I'd decided already that Pease Bay was going to serve as a kind of exile - meaning that I'd quit smoking and drinking and any other vices that hitchhiked on the back of those. Money, or lack thereof, was the main limiting factor. So. I spent most of my first day perched in that window, staring out to sea in the throes of withdrawal, trying to read but slipping slowly in and out of sleep. The second day I headed down to the beach despite the weather not feeling the need to inspire. The bright grey daytime was steeped in perpetual drizzle, which swirled around at the command of the wind, and the red rocks that framed the cove were painted an even deeper shade by the moisture. It was damned near empty that day, besides a small group of indistinguishable figures to my right. I got as close as I could to the sea so that I could listen as it breathed in and out in its trademark meditative breaths. I remember feeling that I'd stepped into some kind of limbo - a place between timelines that I could rest and take stock of my decisions.

Knowing that I couldn't change anything was beside the point.

Have you been to the sea recently? I always forget how much I love it. It's a character trait I copied from a literary character somewhere along the way but I can never remember which one. In fact, it's probably more than one. Besides, what was once a lazy attempt at depth has now become a genuine part of my character. I love the open water and I love how the sand gets a fresh start twice a day. It's inspiring. It helps. I remember hoping in this dumb way that something significant would wash up on the beach as I strode along it. A message in a bottle or an artefact from a long missing aircraft. Any incongruous object would have done the trick. But of course nothing came my way besides the handle of a plastic spade and hundreds of cleaned-out razor clams. I'd taken my shoes off at this point so the latter were particularly irritating.

In my state of meditation I eventually unlocked the part of my brain that I'd been keeping my mother in. Just like that, from nowhere. The memories came in so suddenly that I think I actually stopped myself in my tracks and let the sea come up over my ankles. There was a fresh clarity there all of a sudden, as if the sea had polished a precious gem that I could now thoroughly inspect. Here in front of me was some kind of explanation - this vast mirror that we all emerged from, this place that we could still visit and stare into. My mother was dead, and what I was trying to ignore that whole time was that she was actually gone forever. The patterns of nature were as clear as the tides, and the knowledge that my mother had not gone on to paradise - the knowledge that she had simply gone - was what haunted me so much. It pains me to admit my own selfishness, even after everything we have discussed here tonight, but the reason I could no longer think about my mother was because her death reminded me of my own inescapable fate. And that was what washed up on the beach that day.

That single, lonesome realisation.

I didn't immediately return to Edinburgh. Nor Manchester. Although I would eventually for a brief visit. In fact, that same stroll along the beach still had more to give. You remember me telling you about the small group of people at the head of the beach? Well, as so often happens when you walk along the shore I found myself in their vicinity sooner than I had imagined I would. Before long I was able to hear a loud disagreement that had broken out among them, and it became immediately clear that they were actually two separate groups. I still had my back to them, but I was worried about how close they were getting and stopped being able to enjoy the sea so much. I became aware of how the drizzle had quickly turned to rain, and that there was no way off the beach without coming into contact with the warring factions behind me.

It had spilled over from the caravans.

A woman had been discovered in bed with another man. The other man wasn't even trying to defend himself. Not one excuse left his mouth and everything he said seemed laced with thinly-veiled bluster. His attacker, a man who was shouting now, gave off the impression of massiveness without me even having to face him. His threats came from a primal place that was untouched by logic and driven solely by emotion. I was annoyed at the beach for agreeing to play host to such a barbaric scene, and so I turned around to confront it. The huge man was smaller than I had imagined but was brandishing a kitchen knife. And that's the only word for how he held it. Turned outwards as if already twisting it in somebodies gut. And as luck or fate or destiny would have it I was much closer to the scene than I had previously thought. I made eye contact with the woman as she distanced herself from who I presumed was her husband and I found myself at that crossroads again.

Who's to say what you would do?

The version of me on Arthur's Seat, the version of me on the Royal Mile, and whatever version of myself I currently was hung there in the same moment. The choice was as clear as the ones written in that book there on the table. Turn to page whatever to run away, turn to page forty-something to intervene.

The funny thing about memory is that you're never sure if what you're looking back on is entirely accurate, don't you find? There are memories that you somehow see through the eyes of another person or from an impossible angle, and this is one of them. I can watch myself now, somehow, storming right past the fleeing woman and the bragging man and forcing the full weight of myself through the man with the knife until he folded in two. There was a brief scramble for the knife and one or two sharp blows to my face, but that's all I remember. I don't remember it hurting because I can't quite remember doing it. I remember watching a man prevent a knife attack and I remember the headache I had the day after, but that's about it.

No, really, there's no need to toast to that.

I was barely in charge of my decision. Barely conscious, really. I'd chosen the other path, that which had alluded me twice before, and yet I felt no different. It was clear to me almost immediately, as I walked back up the beach, bloodied but thinking more clearly than ever, that I would still be rewarded by indifference despite what had happened at Pease Bay. The only thing I was unsure about was what I would do with that information now that I had it. So I'll tell you what I did, but only if you agree to take a walk with me. The Man in the Pinstripe Suit is starting to really shout now, and I don't know how long I can stand to sit in an atmosphere like that. He must be drunk, although I do grant you he doesn't look very drunk at all. Oh sure, Eddie has backup. He does this for a living. Plus, I get restless if I stay in one place for too long, don't you? We can loop back around for a nightcap when its blown over. Eddie can fill us in when we get back.

CATHEDRAL

He was really beginning to lose his temper, wasn't he? Definitely not a regular. Eddie did seem to recognise him though, you've got that right. Like I said, probably nothing to worry about. This is Edinburgh, after all. I think we'll see snow if it stays this cold. The sky has turned that special shade of indigo that you don't see very often. But what a time to be alive! This has got to be my favourite part of the evening, with the fire of the last few drinks inside us and the sun disappearing. We'll head down the Royal Mile - I have somewhere in mind that might wrap this evening up for us in the appropriate way. Besides, it'd be nice for you to see a part of Edinburgh that isn't falling to pieces.

It isn't far.

How did I end up living above The Amsterdam, do you mean? Well I suppose that is the question, isn't it. After the incident at Pease Bay I took Hyde - of course I still have him! - He'll be upstairs or prowling this streets for another lost cause, no doubt. I managed to avoid being questioned by the police and made myself scarce pretty quickly, I must admit. I just didn't want to be embroiled in everything. I'd acted on impulse and there was very little else I could offer. An officer on their first day on the force would have been able to tell who was in the wrong, what use would I be?

So we returned to Edinburgh. Me and the cat. It was a horrible day - nothing like tonight - it would have seemed a safe bet to predict it would rain forever. Call it what you want, but suddenly The Amsterdam stood where nothing had stood before. I must have walked past it dozens of times but never looked carefully enough. It looked warm inside, and not so fancy to deny me entry with my unkempt hair and stolen cat hiding inside a duffel bag. My face was a little swollen at this point too, Pease Bay being just the day before, and I wouldn't have been surprised if the looks I was getting had become polite invitations to leave. But Eddie engaged me in conversation, just as he does with everybody.

He told me the room upstairs was free. Told me it wasn't much, but in that old-fashioned way of his that I could work the bar in exchange for rent. If I picked up the odd extra shift then maybe I could earn something on top of that, too. There was something about the challenge of working with alcohol when trying to quit - literally living above temptation - that helped the pieces fall back into place. I was back on track, I felt. Back in the timeline I was supposed to be in.

Thank you, that's very kind.

I do feel much better. Alcohol isn't a problem anymore, in fact, I'm not sure that it ever was. I can drink without it taking me over into the bad place, but I suspect that was all symptomatic of the situation I was in. I'm still not smoking, but feel free to have one yourself now that we're outside. I've even started writing again. There's something in Edinburgh's soul that brings it out of you, I think. Something about that and being alone.

It's a play, actually. There are a few draft copies upstairs if you'd like to-

-You would? I'd really appreciate that. And you promise that's not just the rum talking? You've really been too kind. Really.

Well, here we are. Saint Giles' Cathedral. Magnificent isn't she? And so often neglected by tourists in light of the castle. If we had more light you'd be able to see the spire better, but I suppose we can make do with the stained glass. I always loved the idea of it - you know, how it influences your view of the outside once you're inside. How they only show you what they want you to see. They say a lot about our desire to tell stories, I think. The fact that they're essentially supposed to be functional - to let light in - but still we decide to turn them into tapestries despite glass being perhaps the least welcoming and most delicate of all canvases.

Of course it's closed, it's nearly eleven o'clock! Still, there's no reason that should stop us. It's a public building and it's bloody freezing out here. Nobodies looking! This is the Royal Mile, everyone's either drunk or on a ghost tour, and I've made my opinion on those perfectly clear.

Try the door.

Again.

You're sure? No no, I believe you. Here, let me try.

Don't look so embarrassed, there's a knack to it. Now are you coming in or what? It's all well and good having a look around in the day but there's really something special about a sleeping cathedral. Yes, I'm sure we won't get locked in. Wedge something down there in the door if you want to put your mind at rest - you brought *Journey Beneath The Ice*? - well, use that! You must have had it in your hand this whole time without realising. Eddie'll be on your case...

Now - take it all in for a Second. Isn't it amazing what being inside a massive empty space does to you? This is how we should feel all the time, and yet somehow we block it out. I guess we have to, but it does make me wonder if we're just pretending to be inspired when we look up at the stars to keep us from being so terrified. I feel like we should always be able to hear an echo, do you know what I mean? It's a good job they leave some of the lights on or this would be a whole lot less interesting, wouldn't it.

Well, what do you think?

I know exactly what you mean.

I used to come to church as a kid, with my mother and my grandparents. They were devout Catholics, my grandma and grandad, and the whole thing really was their entire life. Their weeks revolved around going to church and their lives around the definite answer to what would happen to them after they died. My moral code, wether I like it or not, is rooted in Christian ideals. It's easy to roll your eyes at it all - the scope of this building for instance is ridiculous, the stained glass, the golden lectern, the ceiling. But it does inspire introspection. Maybe it's the quiet or the candles, I'm not sure.

There was something inside me that led here when my mother died. I needed something to blame. I needed a reason. But of course there isn't one, not really. It was the last thing I arrived at - after I'd tried to find the same thing in love or art or debauchery. Another facet of life that I hadn't fully explored since an altar boy accidentally hit me in the face with a crucifix when I was a little younger. I know. It was during a ritual called the sections of the cross, in which the priest slowly unveiled different parts of Jesus Christ on this heavy, wooden ornament. In the end you are expected to queue to kiss the feet of Jesus - as a show of faith, I expect. But when my turn came the altar boy slipped a little on the carpeted steps and inadvertently hit me around the face with the heaviest part of the cross. God didn't say a word.

I took that as a sign.

But of course, that's what I'm always looking for. Life is full of symbols. Most people either don't believe in that kind of thing or take no notice. But I do. If a streetlight goes out when I walk under it I feel a sense of dread. Or if I wake up at the same exact time a number of nights in a row I'll start jumping to conclusions. When my mother died I looked for her everywhere, and despite knowing that she'd gone I allowed myself to believe that I'd find her somewhere. I thought she'd leave me a message, you know.

Something.

Because that's my religion. Coincidence is my God. The interconnectedness of everything. Because without that, what else do we have? I hope I haven't given you the impression that I'm hopeless, and maybe that's why I brought you here. I've been lost, sure, but who among us hasn't been? There have been moments when I've wanted to give up, or when I've rebelled against my nature because things hadn't been going my way. Of course I wasn't being rewarded for being a nice person by some omnipresent being. Of course - and it pains me to admit this - I'm not the protagonist in some grand interwoven narrative. Look, I couldn't even bring myself to save those people. I've shown cowardice, and more recently I've made steps towards redeeming myself. But I'm slowly coming to terms with my insignificance. Buildings like this are a shrine to that feeling, and no matter how stubborn or misguided the people who built them were, they were still trying to coax meaning out of the meaningless. They were trying.

Now, should we light a fucking candle and get out of here?
They're over there, in the corner. I've done it since I was a kid but I'm not exactly sure why. My family taught me to light them for loved

THE HYPOCRITE

ones - in a sort of tribute - but I think I always thought of them as another version of throwing coins into the bottom of a well. Making a wish inside a church surely makes it more viable, no?

Even if we did break in.

There's no need to keep looking over your shoulder, honestly. Nobody saw us.

Do you have a lighter? I'll light mine off of yours. My mother used to sort of stand there for a while afterwards, praying I guess, watching the flame. But I think we can just stand here quietly for a minute. I'm starting to get sick of the sound of my own voice, anyway.

***

ANTONY SZMIEREK

***

Are you okay?

Sometimes we just need a minute to think. How do you feel about a nightcap? Before we go our separate ways. We can stick another few tunes on the jukebox, can't we? That is, if The Man in the Pinstripe Suit hasn't burned The Amsterdam to the ground. Oh, and don't forget the book you wedged in the door. I'd rather not live through the ending where we get locked in until morning.

HYPOTHESIS

The door is usually locked at this point in the night… he must really be distracted.

Eddie?

Oh, okay. Full blown argument now. Listen, let's just sit down over here and give him some support from a distance. Just so he knows we're here. Look, he's spotted us. Just over here, Eddie. Okay mate? He'll be fine I'm sure. So much for that nightcap though, I hardly fancy approaching the bar. I suppose we saw this coming in one way or another, didn't we?

That's a good question. I've been wondering when you were going to ask that. It's understandable that you'd think I wasn't being entirely sincere. I mean, is it possible for anybody to be entirely sincere or am I just trying to get something out of this? Maybe I am, but that's not something you need to worry about. A conversation goes two ways. Both of us are still here because we are getting something out of this. You probably entertained my ramblings in the first place because you were alone and found me somewhat entertaining. You probably wanted to laugh at me, secretly, or just remember the stranger parts of the conversation to share as an anecdote with your real friends later down the line. And hey - who's saying that you won't still do that? But I'm not trying to con you, honestly. There are no stooges here, no mirrors or deceit. Just two strangers having a nightcap in a bar. Let's toast to you, this time. Even without drinks it still counts. For listening. For remaining suspicious. For coming along for the ride.

In truth this is just where I've ended up. I'm still searching for meaning and have in no way found anything that could pass for an acceptable answer. Every conclusion I reach is countered with something equally as plausible, but I have arrived somewhere.

I've arrived at a hypothesis.

I don't have any children, and so these musings would be dead on arrival if I didn't share them with the people I meet. I think that is where it all comes from - my writing, Mezzanine, Simone and Owen. I'm desperate to connect, to share my experiences with those who will listen and maybe find something valuable in return. A rebuttal of my theories, perhaps. The chance for somebody to prove me wrong or evidence that I've been pointlessly meandering through my life with nothing to show for it. On a basic level it boils down to one contradiction - Am I doing this to feel valued or am I doing this to help? Am I a transmitter or just a receiver? To distil it further, are we all just inherently selfish?

If they get any louder we should start thinking about going over there to help, shouldn't we? Can you make out what they're arguing about, at all? Money, for sure. Some names I'm unfamiliar with. I'm baffled that he's not called me over - he must want this to somehow remain private. I'd argue that they were family if they even looked slightly alike, but I can't stretch to it.

I'm nearly finished, you needn't look so anxious. Now, as you sip your drink you will no doubt be thinking of your own regrets, and weighing them up against your achievements. Focus on me, please. This is the important part. But you'll never reach an equilibrium, not if you're really honest with yourself. These last years of my life, the ones you've listened so generously to, have been a search for a cure to selfishness. I've been thinking that in some way it could be love. Romantic love is rarely selfless of course, but it can have its moments. People refusing to leave the bedside of their sick partners for example, or those who sacrifice their own life to save that of a loved one. But maybe, secretly, as they cut their own rope and plummet to certain death in alligator-infested waters, they're thinking of the tributes to them that will play out on the news the following day. The wreaths, the tears, and the celebrity eulogies. Maybe.

You're still listening, aren't you?

Eddie will be fine.

Just listen.

My mother died selfishly. The surgical enhancements she had paid for were risky and frivolous, but I'll always respect her acknowledgement of that. She knew how ridiculous the whole thing was at her age, but she told the odds to fuck off and did it anyway. My mother spat in the face of her own hypocrisy and I'll always love her for it. I'll always love her in that completely unselfish way a son can love his mother. So, when you walked in here tonight, just like I did after my trip to the beach with nothing but a stolen cat and some pointless artefacts in a duffel bag, I thought I'd share with you what I've learned so that you don't make the same mistakes everyone else makes. The same mistakes I made. You can't control life, mate, but you can control your response to it.

Focus.

All we can do is try our best. We're all out here trying to solve a puzzle that we don't even have all the pieces to. Mold has gotten at the box and obscured the picture we're trying to make, and of course because it's second-hand a toddler has bitten off the edges of most of the pieces, or smushed them up in its gums so that they've become papier-mâché. What chance do we have? Well, I think we still play the game because trying is a whole lot more fun than sitting it out. You just have to find your place, that's all. If you're not beautiful then be funny. If you're not funny then use your intellect. If you're not logical, create. Compete. Better yourself. But be kind as you do. Find someone to love and you'll be loved in return. You have to be selfish sometimes in order to give people your best, that's all. It's standard procedure on flights for a reason. You know, the whole 'secure your oxygen mask first before helping others' thing. That's the way we should look at it. We're all hypocrites, but that's what makes us so interesting. It's a beautiful word really, hypocrite, and it doesn't even really mean what we think it does. It's a combination of the Greek 'hypo', which means 'under', and the verb 'krinein' - I think I said that right? - which means to sift, or to decide. So it's original meaning only implied a deficiency in the ability to decide, so, well... isn't that all of us? How can we decide what we are if we don't know why we're here? Hypocrisy is necessary. It's confusion. It's the best word we have to describe why we all feel so connected. We should really have toasted to the Greeks.

Now it's time for you to choose.

Concentrate on me, please. I apologise if I'm being forceful, and I apologise for having to raise my voice, it's just those two at the bar are really going for each other, aren't they? Look, most people are selfish, I've told you that. The world around them is poisoned with racism, sexism, war, poverty and disease, and they do absolutely nothing to help because it doesn't directly affect them. This is your chance.

The Man in the Pinstripe Suit has a knife in his pocket. Earlier we heard it drop to the ground and I saw it with my own eyes as I sat at the bar. Now, I'm going to leave it up to you to intervene, or to let this happen. I've told you my hypothesis and now it's up to you prove or disprove it. If you flee Eddie could die, but you won't. You'll live and the universe will be just as indifferent to you as it currently is. Or you can run over there and overpower The Man in the Pinstripe Suit, send the knife flying, and save Eddie's life. That's your choice. But again - the universe will be just as indifferent to you as it currently is. That won't change. I guess the question I'm asking you is this - do you still see the point in trying? Even after everything I've told you? Of course I didn't plan this! As I've just said, you can't control life but you can control your response to it. I'm a teacher, remember? I'm trying to help you. Now, unless your choice is complete inaction, your time is quickly running out.

    Turn to page something or other to save Eddie.

    Turn to page whatever to escape.

    Your choice.

    Don't look at me like that! This isn't my problem!

    He's begging for help. Come on! I can see the knife.

    Turn the page.

    Make a choice, for goodness sake!

Printed in Poland
by Amazon Fulfillment
Poland Sp. z o.o., Wrocław